CHARIS   NEWBERRY
CHRISTMAS

Text copyright © 1989 by Anne-Marie Dalmais
Illustration copyright © 1989 by Violayne Hulné
English translation copyright © 1989 OBC., Inc.
All rights reserved.

This 1989 edition published by Derrydale Books,
distributed by Crown Publishers, Inc.
225 Park Avenue South, New York,
New York 10003.

ISBN - 0 - 517 - 66276 - 0
h g f e d c b a

Library of Congress Cataloging-in-Publication Data
Dalmais, Anne-Marie, 1954.
Best bedtime stories of Mother Pig / by Anne-Marie Dalmais.
p. 32, cm 19,5 x 25,5
Summary: Presents two stories within a story, as Mother Pig
relates bedtimes tales to soothe her piglets to sleep.
ISBN 0-517-66276-0
1. Children's stories, French-Translations into English.
2. Children's stories, English-Translations from French.
(1. Pigs-Fiction. 2. Short stories). I. Title.
PZ7.D166Bdh 1988 - (E) - dc19 - 88-10861 CIP AC

THE BEST BEDTIME STORIES

OF MOTHER PIG

Stories by Anne-Marie Dalmais
illustrated by Violayne Hulné

English translation by DIANE COHEN

DERRYDALE BOOKS
New York

To get to her own bedroom, Mother Pig must go straight past the room where her little ones sleep. She has done this so many times that by now she can make her way with her eyes closed. But this evening she stops suddenly in the middle of the hallway, surprised by an unusual silence.

Not one sound is coming from her children's room - not a murmur, not a whisper, not even the tiniest giggle! "They must be up to something!" thinks Mother Pig as she flings open the door. Amazing! The room is empty, completely empty! The only clue to where the missing children might be is a tell-tale chair, pulled up to the window. Her three piglets have escaped to the garden! And there, in the moonlight, they're picking handful after handful of delicious strawberries, raspberries, and currants!

Mother Pig is very angry! She leans out of the window and calls down to the garden, "That's enough, you little rascals! Come inside this instant! You naughty, naughty children! You will have to be punished. I will not tell you any stories before you go to sleep tonight!" The children come sheepishly back to the house.

The two brothers, with berry-stained faces, don't feel very proud of themselves. They sigh deep, sorry sighs.

But their sister keeps smiling. She offers her mother all the fruits she has picked wrapped in a large cabbage leaf. Then in her sweet, charming voice, she says, "Mother, dear Mother, your little pigs beg your forgiveness!"

Mother Pig cannot stay mad after this fine performance and gives in with a little smile. Sighing, she sits down on a bench and utters the words they've been waiting for so eagerly: "Once upon a time..."

A Topsy-Turvy Day

Once upon a time there was a little pig named Bow-Tie because he always wore around his neck a delicate bow tie made of silk. He lived in the city with his parents, in a house surrounded by a small garden. He had a younger sister named Rose, but since she was still only a baby, he couldn't really play with her. Instead he was happy to entertain her by putting on puppet shows above her crib.

One Tuesday morning, Bow-Tie's alarm clock does not ring and his topsy-turvy day begins. "Blockhead!" Bow-Tie says to the clock in a huff. (In fact, he's the blockhead. He forgot to set it the night before!)

"Hurry up, Bow-Tie," his mother calls. "You're going to be late for school! Why are you still in bed?"

Hop! Bow-Tie jumps into his clothes!
Hop! Hop! He straps on his school bag and books!
Hop! Hop! Hop! He races down the stairs and leaves without eating his favorite breakfast of toast and honey. What a way to start the day!

10

Phew! Bow-Tie gets to school just before the bell rings. His stomach is empty, but he has arrived right on time! He has barely caught his breath when his grammar teacher asks to see his workbook. Oh no! Our little pig has left it at home. Both his books have blue covers and he picked up the wrong one because he was in a hurry. "You scatterbrain! You'll stay after school!" scolds Mr. Dictionary.

Recess at last! A good game of ball will help him forget about the morning's troubles. But unlucky Bow-Tie trips over a stone and falls flat on his nose!

The little pig finds himself in a daze. In the nurse's office, he's given first aid and big bandages for his scratches and scrapes.

To make matters worse, the nurse forbids him to go swimming in the afternoon. "Please," he pleads, "swimming is my favorite sport. Bad luck is following me!" sighs Bow-Tie, sulking.

Nevertheless, since he loves to eat, he's hoping that lunch will make him feel better after all these mishaps.
But it is not to be. Today the cafeteria is serving a meal he simply cannot stand — awful, boiled leeks and terrible, stewed prunes.

Miss Goody-Goody, the goose who patrols the lunchroom, catches the little pig making faces and says to him, "Bow-Tie, please, don't be finicky. You must eat some lunch."
His friends burst out laughing when they see him brooding and tease him, "Eat up, old pal!"

Luckily the afternoon begins with a penmanship exercise, our little student's favorite subject. His face brightens with a big smile.

He takes out his trusty pen, the one with the very soft tip, and his notebook with the double-lined paper. Bow-Tie is ready to practice. He can't wait to get started!

It's so much fun to write the pretty letters on the clean, white page, to round off the "o's" perfectly, to elongate the "l's" delicately, to zigzag with the "z's" and to neatly dot the "i's". Bow-Tie works very happily.

But suddenly, without warning, his favorite pen starts to screech, cough, and spit. Then zoom! It shoots a long stream of black ink that splatters the entire page with a big, awful, dark spot. Poor Bow-Tie. Now he's afraid he'll fail for sure.

And this isn't the end of his problems! In the afternoon, on the way home from school, he hears an awful ripping sound behind him, and suddenly, the strap of his knapsack tears apart!

His mother had told him many times not to put too many things in this cloth bag. But it's really no fun to carry all your books balanced on one shoulder!

15

At home, the problems continued for poor Bow-Tie. When he goes to kiss his sister hello, she grabs his silk tie, pulling apart the bow, and then grabs it away, shrieking with joy! She's just like a pirate with her loot!

But Bow-Tie isn't going to give up his beloved tie. He snatches it back and tries to redo the double knot. But he has trouble retying it and now Rose is crying and crying, making him very nervous.

Then, at the worst possible moment, the next-door neighbor, Mrs. Meddler, arrives. Bow-Tie doesn't like her one bit because every time she visits she smothers him with kisses. Then she teases him about how chubby he's getting to be.

This day has been too much! After such an avalanche of adversity, such a downpour of disasters and disappointments, and this shower of minor mishaps, poor Bow-Tie has only one wish left: to get into bed and fall asleep right away. He wants to forget all the calamities of this tumultuous Tuesday!

When his mother, the kind Mrs. Pot-Roast, comes upstairs to say, "Good night" he doesn't hear her because he's already asleep, far away in dreamland...

A Fanciful Christmas

Once upon a time there were two twin brothers, two identical little pigs. One was called Trixie and the other was called Taffie. They resembled each other in every way: each had the same chubby face, the same turned-up muzzle, and the same plump shape. But their personalities were completely opposite. Quiet and sweet, Taffie was a model of obedience, while feisty Trixie was always inventing one harebrained scheme after another and searching for adventure from morning to night.

One Christmas our twins and their parents travel to the family cabin in the country for a holiday vacation. Each of the piglets has invited his best friend. Trixie has chosen Jester, a chattering little goose who loves to play practical jokes. And Taffie brings along Cupcake, a gentle and helpful puppy.

The four friends share a bedroom made entirely out of wood, with neat little beds built deep into the wall so they look like cupboards, even better, secret caves!

Trixie and Jester are the first to go upstairs. Together, these two mischief-makers sew up the legs of Cupcake's and Taffie's pajamas. When the others go to put them on, they can't figure out what happened.

The next day, the twins and their friends take a walk in the pine forest with Mr. Fa-La-La, who asks them, "Which of these trees do you think is the most beautiful?" They decide, for fun, to make a game out of answering. They decide to give the trees a grade from 1 to 10, in order of their beauty. "This one gets an 8!" they say. "I'll give this one a 3!" they decide. "Oh, this is definitely a 10!" they exclaim. "And this one over here looks like a 7 to me!" they finish, laughing.

The following day is Christmas Eve! There's a feeling of mystery and excitement throughout the house.

Trixie secretly draws a picture for his parents. His brother and his friends are quick to do the same.

Once all the works of art are completed, Taffie — patient and careful Taffie — puts himself in charge of rolling up the drawings and decorating them with a brilliant bow made of satin ribbon.

Then the little goose silently creeps downstairs to slip the fragile gifts underneath the flight of stairs.

On his way, Jester notices a sign on the kitchen door absolutely forbidding anyone to enter that room. For it is there, in the magical domain of Mrs. Fa-La-La, that the grandest and most beautiful surprises are being prepared!

In the evening, Trixie, Taffie, Jester, and Cupcake eat supper on a tray in their room, munching and nibbling on delicious crispy toast with jam and butter.

After this delicious meal, Taffie and Cupcake go to bed like good little children. Trixie and Jester, on the other hand, sneak away...

They take with them a flashlight so they won't wake anyone by turning on a light. The two make their way ever so quietly down the stairs, step by step, on tippy toe, like two little thieves.

Suddenly they hear Mr. Fa-La-La cough in his room, and Jester panics! Losing his nerve, the little goose abandons his friend and runs back upstairs to bed as fast as he can waddle.

Trixie continues on his journey alone. This little mischief-maker wants to see what's hidden behind the forbidden door! He is so curious, so impatient, that he simply cannot wait until morning. He just wants to take a peek, one teeny-weeny peek, and then he'll go back to bed.

He opens the door just a crack... and discovers an enchanting sight! The entire room is illuminated by the silvery moonlight. In the center, in the place of honor, is the most beautiful pine tree from the forest, transported there as if by magic, and adorned with glittering decorations that make it even more fantastic.

Trixie is entranced. He cannot take his eyes off the bewitching sight. He goes in and sits in a chair, looking and looking at this wonderful tree. But soon everything begins to look soft and blurry, the garlands dance round and round in a circle, and the decorations first grow larger and then smaller. Our little pig can no longer stay awake and soon he falls asleep with a mixture of wonder and delight on his face.

An hour later, his father comes downstairs to get a glass of water and finds him fast asleep. Of course, Mr. Fa-La-La has known all along that Trixie had disobeyed, but, touched by his happy and innocent expression, he gently takes him in his arms and carries him upstairs to bed. The feel of the cool sheets awakens the piglet for an instant. He no longer knows where he has been. The beautiful, sparkling tree has disappeared. Did he really go down to the kitchen or had he dreamed it all ? He doesn't wonder for very long because his eyes close again... and then he is asleep...

Mother Pig's three little children have done the same. They, too, don't really know if they have heard, or dreamed, this story about a Christmas dream. But as they sleep, they see lovely visions of Christmas trees decorated with surprises and of delectable delicacies and fascinating mirages of glorious gifts and feast...

Their sleep is blissful and calm, and beneath the canopy of their huge old bed, they begin to snore peacefully and evenly, one at a time, echoing each other, or sometimes all three together.

Mother Pig delights in the full, deep sound of this customary and welcome refrain. It's the sweet, reassuring accompaniment to a good and restful night.